Maggie and Shine

by Luanne
Armstrong

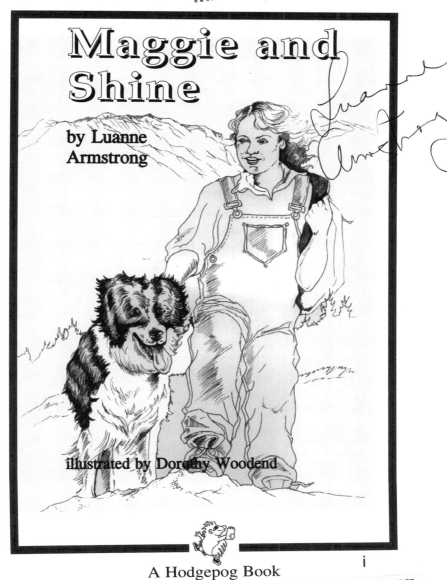

illustrated by Dorothy Woodend

A Hodgepog Book

i

Hodgepog Books and The Books Collective acknowledge the ongoing support of the Canada Council for the Arts and Alberta Foundation for the Arts for our publishing program. We also acknowledge the support of the City of Edmonton and Edmonton Arts Council.

Editors for Press:
Mary Woodbury, Glen Huser

Cover design by Robert Woodbury
Inside Layout by Dianne Cooper at The Books Collective
in CG Times, Palatino, Arial and Times New Roman (True-Type Font)
in Windows Quark X-Press 4.0.
Printed at Hignell Press

A Hodgepog Book for Kids

Published in Canada by Hodgepog Books, a member of:
The Books Collective,
214-21 10405 Jasper Avenue,
Edmonton, Alberta, T5J 3S2.
Telephone (780) 448 0590

Canadian Cataloguing in Publishing Data
Armstrong, Luanne, 1949-
 Maggie and Shine

ISBN 1895836-67-0

1. Dogs--Juvenile fiction. I.Woodend, Dorothy 1968- II. Title
PS8551.R7638M34 1999   jC813'.54   C99-910698-8
PZ7.A7638Ma 1999

Thank you:
Thanks to my helpful readers,
Hannah Rose, Margie Jamieson,
Kaca Hegerova, and Dorothy
Armstrong. Thanks as well to
Kinmont Willie, who sighs with
impatience every time I sit down to
write and makes it plain that he
wishes his owner would get a real
job herding sheep somewhere.

Dedicated, with much love, to
Hannah and Gaelin

Table of Contents

Chapter One

Maggie held her breath and held on to her seat belt as the truck swayed around another steep corner. She looked out the window. She could see right over the edge of the road, down to the river running white and foaming in the crack of the valley far below. The truck was too close to the edge, she thought. She held her breath. She was sitting by the door, and her mother was sitting next to her father, who was driving their loaded truck and camper up the narrow twisted logging road into the mountains.

Suddenly her father whooped, "Maggie. Look there! See, it's an elk."

Reluctantly, Maggie looked up. The elk was standing in the road, staring at the strange apparition of the loaded truck and camper growling its way up the hill. Suddenly, the elk leapt to the side of the road, over the ditch and into the brush.

"Yahoo! Run, girl," laughed her father.

"Oh, it was so beautiful," said her mother. "Are there a lot of elk up here, Len?"

"Sure," he said. "Lots of everything, deer, elk, bears, maybe even a few cougar. We're leaving civilization behind for a while. Just be us and the animals, Jo."

"And a thousand sheep," said Maggie's mother sharply. "I wonder if we should stop and check on the dogs. They might need a drink."

"They're fine," said her dad impatiently. "We've still got a lot of mountain to climb. Eh, Maggie? What do you think of it, way up here. Sure is beautiful, isn't it?"

"I hate it," Maggie said. "It's horrible. I can see right over the side of the road. Down to the river. It's really steep! What if we fall off?"

Her dad laughed. "Hey, you think that's steep. Wait until we get up a little higher. Then it gets really steep. Hey, you scared? What about that, Jo, our brave Maggie is scared."

"Of course she is, Len," said her mother sharply. "And just keep your eyes on the road. That drop would make anyone nervous."

Maggie folded her arms tight around herself. She wanted to close her eyes but she was too nervous. None of this was her idea. If she had her way, they'd all be back home, safe in their own house, and she'd be playing with her friends. That's what summer was supposed to be for. She felt tears start in her eyes and

2

she squeezed them back. She wasn't going to cry. Her dad would only tease her some more. She tried to stop staring down at the river. In her imagination, she kept seeing the truck wheels sliding over the edge of the road. She looked up at the mountain instead. Maybe she would see another elk or a deer, or even a bear.

Her father and mother had taken a course at the local college to learn how to be sheepherders. They had a farm where they grew raspberries and peaches, but the farm never seemed to make enough money. A summer spent sheepherding would pay well. Maggie's dad had gone to Appleby one day and come home with two black and white dogs in the truck.

"I rented these dogs from another sheepherder. These are border collies," he had explained to Maggie. "This kind of dog has been used for centuries to herd sheep. This dog's name is Rex, and this girl here is Shine. They are going to be our helpers for the summer. But don't get too attached to them. They're workers, not pets."

He gestured with his hand and both dogs lay down on the ground, staring at him with their brown eyes. They seemed to be watching his every move.

"C'mon, team," he said, "let's go meet the real boss," and the dogs leapt up again, and followed him into the house. Maggie went with them. They used to have a dog, a beautiful golden retriever named Boo, but he had gotten old and one day her parents had taken Boo to Dr. Ross, the veterinarian, and he hadn't come home. Maggie had missed having a dog to go with her on her rambles around the farm, through the woods, or down to the beach. She bent over to scratch behind their ears. Rex licked her nose and Shine wiggled her body all over, so that it seemed like she

was laughing silently. They both laid down and stared intensely at Maggie.

"These are very highly-trained dogs," her dad said sternly. "Maggie, you can start this summer, learning to work with them. We'll all make a great team."

"But I want to stay here." Maggie was furious. "I don't want to go live on some dumb old mountain. What about my friends, and the beach? What am I supposed to do while you're chasing after a bunch of dumb sheep?"

"Our family is a team," her father said sternly. "We stick together and help each other."

"This isn't helping me," Maggie yelled. "It's not helping me to be stuck on a stupid mountain somewhere, with none of my friends and nothing to do."

"Maggie," said her mother and father together.

"Yelling doesn't solve anything," her mother said. "We've tried to teach you to solve problems by communicating." Maggie looked at her mother's stern face. Her mom had brown eyes and long brown hair tied in a ponytail. Maggie liked to do things with her mom. Her mom always had ideas for food to cook, pictures to draw, or crafts to make. She almost never lost her temper. But now she looked angry.

Maggie sighed and shrugged. She'd heard this speech before. She could practically recite it. She was sure it would be lonely up in the mountains. It sounded so different from anything she knew. She would miss her friends, Ben and Brad, who lived next door. They had spent their summer together for as long as she could remember, riding their bikes, swimming and fishing in the nearby lake, going to the local burger stand for ice cream. When she told them she would be gone all summer, Ben said, "You mean, there's like no houses, no stores, no ice cream, no movies? Wow, gross."

Brad said, "But we always do stuff together in the summer. Who will we play with? That's so dumb."

She didn't say anything more to her parents. She went to her room and lay on her bed and stared at the wall. If she tried to say how she really felt, her parents would only start lecturing about the value of work, and how important it was to contribute to the family. If she kept on trying to say what she wanted, they'd give her another speech about respect and manners. She sighed. Sometimes she hated being an only child. When her parents started lecturing, there was only her, standing there, forced to listen. Now she would be with them all summer, with no possibility of escape. Maybe she could run away. But how could she find her way in the mountains by herself? Living in the mountains was going to be terrifying. Oh great, scared and bored at the same time.

She hadn't thought too much about all the wild animals she might see. But now her father had said there might be bears. And cougars! She wasn't afraid of wild animals while she was here in the truck with her parents, the bright sun beating down on the dark trees and tangled brush. But she wondered what it would be like at night, when they were all living in the camper, and someone had to go outside with the dogs to check on the sheep.

After what seemed hours of driving through the dust and over the steep bumpy gravel road, the truck ground to a halt beneath a grove of thick dark trees.

Len switched off the engine. "We're here," he announced happily. "Home sweet home."

"Brr," Jo said. "I'm tired and stiff and hungry. And I'll bet you are too, Maggie. Let's get a fire going, make a nice cup of tea, and see what we want for supper."

Len let the dogs out of the camper. They began running around, sniffing everything, wagging their tails at all the new smells.

Reluctantly, Maggie got out of the truck. She shivered as she looked around. It was freezing here. Where was her cozy room, her warm bed? She went and sat on a log, her arms wrapped around each other.

"I thought there was supposed to be a bunch of dumb sheep," Maggie muttered.

"What's that, Maggie?" her father said. He was chopping wood. He had a big goofy smile on his face. "Oh, the sheep. They're over in another valley," he said.

Why did he have to be so cheerful? Couldn't he tell she was cold and tired and scared.

"They'll be bringing them over tomorrow. In the meantime, we've got to get our camp set up and get ready to go to work. Once the sheep get here, someone has to watch them all the time. Isn't that right, gang?" he said to the dogs.

Maggie stood up, sauntered over, got a comic book out of the truck. She sat on a log reading while her parents started a fire and began to make supper. They kept looking at her and then at each other. She could see them over the edge of the page.

"Why don't you go explore a bit, Maggie?" said her mother. "It's beautiful here."

"Yeah, c'mon, honey," said her father."Get your head out of that stupid comic and come with your old dad." He grabbed her hand and pulled her up from her seat on the log. She dragged her feet and stumbled after him through the trees.

He stopped. "Look at that, eh!" he said. "Wow, that's really something. This place is amazing."

Their camp was on a flat piece of ground which overlooked a huge opening full of baby trees. Beyond the opening was a black wall of forest and beyond that, a ring of craggy mountains. The snow still lingering on these peaks was just turning pink in the last rays of the setting sun. They glowed with a rosy fire. Even grumpy as she was, Maggie knew it was beautiful. But she didn't have to admit it out loud.

"I'm cold," she grumbled."Can we go back to the fire?"

"That big open patch is called a clearcut," her father lectured enthusiastically, as if he hadn't heard her at all. Maggie wished he would stay quiet and let her take in the view.

"The sheep eat the weeds and brush to let the new baby trees grow. Our job is to protect the sheep, keep them from grazing too much in one place and not enough in others. That's why the dogs are so important; they protect the sheep, round them up, help us move them from place to place."

A creek was tumbling down through the trees near the campsite. Flowers bloomed everywhere. "It's like a giant garden," she thought. Maybe this summer

8

wouldn't be so absolutely terrible after all. She certainly would have lots of adventures to tell her friends when she went back to school. They had all felt so sorry for her. They'd be so glad when she returned, when they saw she had survived this terrible summer.

The dogs barked. Something big and heavy crashed away through the brush. Maggie couldn't see what it was. Shine came running back from wherever she had been and stared up at Maggie and her father with her intense brown eyes. She looked back at the brush and then nudged Maggie with her nose.

"Good girl, Shine," said her father. "You guard Maggie. That's your job."

Maggie shivered. It was time to get back to the warmth of fire, and the good smells of food cooking. Then tonight, she would sleep in the camper, safe from all the wild animals. She would be in her new warm sleeping bag, curled up with her favourite stuffed toy, an old grey elephant, which she'd brought with her in secret just for comfort. If her parents knew, they'd laugh at her for being a baby. She'd also smuggled into the camper several of her favourite books, a heap of *Spiderman* and *Bone* comics, and a stash of chocolate bars, just for emergencies. Just the same, it was going to be a long summer.

That night, Maggie lay awake. She tossed and turned, trying to sleep. Her parents were snoring away in the double bed below her. There was a tiny window by her bed. She opened it.

From far away, she could hear the wind in the trees. It sounded like far-away waves crashing on a beach. The creek rushing down the mountain gurgled and whispered as if it were talking to itself.

Her favourite way to get to sleep at night was daydreaming of the great adventures she would have when she was grown up. Tonight she decided to make up a story for herself as a great mountain climber, winning prizes and being cheered by huge crowds of people. Slowly she drifted to sleep to the sounds of their happy applause.

Chapter Two

Sheepherding was hard work, Maggie thought. She hadn't known what to expect. By now the sheep had been in the valley for a week. For the first few days, Maggie had stayed near the fire, reading the same dumb old comic, or huddled sulking in the camper. But when her father asked her once more to go with him to help with the sheep, she decided she was bored enough to try anything. She watched him work with Rex and Shine. Like tiny black and white streaks, the dogs ran around the edge of the sheep herd, responding to her father's whistles and hand gestures. They stood up, crouched, lay flat, crept forward, never taking their eyes off the sheep. Maggie's dad was always busy. There was always something to do, a sheep which needed help, or a lamb which had lost its mother.

For the first few days, Maggie watched him and followed him around. After a while she brought a book with her and lay in the warm sun. Then she began to spend some time looking around and exploring. The mountain valley in which they were camped was the most beautiful place she had ever seen. There were so many flowers, gold and blue and red and purple. The mountain peaks had big patches of ice and snow, towering cliffs and black crooked trees. There was a tiny lake in the middle of the valley. The tumbling creek fell down the mountain into the lake.

"In the winter, this valley is under ten feet of snow," said her father. "Summer is short up here in the alpine area. Everything has to grow fast before snow comes again." He knew a lot about the plants and animals. He showed her the little piles of grass cut by the picas or rock rabbits and left to dry in the sun. Marmots whistled at her from the rocks.

Usually the sun shone, but almost every day, clouds blew in for a brief while and then blew away again. Once Maggie's father took her to the edge of the valley and she watched in astonishment as clouds climbed up the mountains towards them. The clouds were cold and wet. Soon it was raining and Maggie was glad to go back to the safety and warmth of the trailer. But the rain was brief and, as soon as it was over, the sun was shining again.

"You can have snow here anytime," her father said. "Always take a coat and matches with you when

13

you leave the camper. Be prepared for anything." He showed her how to build a fire using a jackknife, shavings, wax from candle, and matches. He also gave her a whistle. "Never go too far from camp," he warned. "This place is beautiful but it can be dangerous for anyone, no matter how smart they are. You should always be prepared for anything."

Every day the sheep spread out over the valley to graze and, at night, the dogs brought them in close to the camper where they lay down to sleep for the night. Maggie's parents had put up a tent, built a fireplace out of rocks, hung up ropes for clotheslines. The camp was a cozy place. They got their drinking and cooking water from the stream and went there every morning and evening to wash in the freezing cold water. Maggie's mother cooked over the fire, even though they had a propane stove in the camper. Maggie was beginning to think this new life wasn't as bad as she had pictured. She missed her friends back in the valley, and their usual summer activities, like going for ice cream, or riding their bikes. But the valley had begun to seem far away.

When she was sitting in the sun in the afternoons, watching the flowers blow and dance in the wind, often Shine would come and sit with her. Maggie was fascinated by Shine's careful attention to everything that was going on. She would lie down, her eyes on the sheep, her fuzzy black and white ears twitching and turning with every noise. Her eyes were like bright brown buttons, with yellow lights deep inside.

Sometimes her eyes would close and she would appear to be asleep, but the slightest noise would bring her back to attention. Sometimes something Maggie couldn't see or hear would send her on a flashing patrol, her quick tiny feet pattering like mad around the edge of the sheep herd. She would return,

flop down with a heavy sigh, and go back to her watch. Maggie laughed at how she would lie with her hind legs stretched out behind her, and her front paws crossed over each other.

"It's what they are trained for, and they take their job seriously," her dad had explained. "They were first bred in England and Scotland to help the shepherds on the moors. They are very smart and very fast. But Shine really seems to like you, Maggie. I've noticed she always goes to find you. I think she wants to be your friend."

Maggie thought so too. She liked both Rex and Shine, but Rex spent his time with her father. Shine always came to find Maggie. But she didn't want to get too attached to Shine. Her dad said they would have to give the dogs back at the end of the summer. They were only rented. It seemed a funny idea, renting dogs.

One night, Maggie was awakened by a noise outside the camper. It was a yipping, howling shrieking noise. The dogs barked furiously, then she heard their feet thud on the ground as they rushed off. Maggie sat up in bed, her heart in her throat.

"Coyotes," said her dad, waking up. "They won't bother the sheep with the dogs around. But I'd better go check." He threw on a coat and went outside. Maggie and her mother lay awake until he came back.

"No problem," he said. "But that Shine. What a dog. She just never relaxes. I wonder if she ever sleeps? She was right there, ready to take on all those coyotes all by herself. Rex always stays behind her. I guess he thinks she's the big boss."

The next morning, Maggie's father said, "Since Shine and you get along so well, Maggie, why don't you work with her a bit. This morning, you can patrol with her, and I'll show you some of the signals and commands you need to use."

Maggie's stomach did a flip-flop. What if she did something wrong? But Shine seemed glad to have her company and, when Maggie gave the arm wave that sent her on patrol, she took off like a little blur, then returned to sit panting at Maggie's feet. Sometimes Shine would wrinkle her lips and show her teeth.

"She's smiling," said Maggie's father. "She's smiling at you."

"Good girl," said Maggie hesitantly. "Good dog."

"Well, you're doing fine on your own," her father said. "I have something I need at the camper. I'll be back soon." Her father went off and left them alone. Maggie felt very grown up and important, and a little scared, standing on a flower-covered hill with Shine at her side, watching over a thousand grazing sheep, keeping them safe.

She was getting to know the sheep now. She was beginning to be able to tell them apart. In her mind, she had started giving them names: Curly, Twisted Ear, Blackface, Soreleg. Now that they were used to her, they accepted her presence along with that of the dogs and Maggie's father.

Whenever the sheep were frightened of anything, they crowded together. Maggie's father had a long stick with a curled end which he called a shepherd's crook. He used it to direct the sheep. Sometimes, if he needed to catch one, he hooked the stick around the sheep's neck. He showed Maggie how a sheep would stop struggling and go limp when it was turned on its back. Maggie laughed. An upside down sheep was a foolish-looking animal.

Chapter Three

"Hey, crew! Everybody up! Get up!" shouted Maggie's father joyfully. "Time to move. Sun's up. Time to get to work."

"Oh, Len, how can you be so cheerful in the morning?" groaned Maggie's mother. "Go make the coffee and let me and Maggie sleep."

"I'm up, Dad," said Maggie, jumping out of her bunk. Her dad slammed the camper door and went outside, whistling. It was moving day, time to move the sheep and the camper to a new grazing area.

"It's the gypsy life, Jo, my love," her dad said, clomping back into the camper with a steaming mug of coffee. He started whistling and jumping around on the camper floor in a silly dance. Maggie sighed. Sometimes her dad didn't even seem like a grown up. His hair was getting longer this summer and he had started wearing it in a ponytail. This morning, he had on torn blue jeans, an old sweatshirt, and hiking boots.

"I'm a farmer," Jo said disapprovingly, "not a gypsy. I like my roots in the ground, in one place."

"Well, today you're going to be a lady trucker. You'll have to navigate the truck over the pass to Rainbow Creek. I got a map from Forestry. It should be all right."

"Maggie can stay with me," Jo said. "She can help me navigate."

"Oh, oh," Len said. "I told her she could help move the sheep. She's been doing such a good job with Shine. They're really getting along well. She's turning into a great little shepherd. I was right. We're going to make a great team."

"Oh, Len, I need her. I can't drive all that way by myself. What if something goes wrong?"

"You've got the radio in the truck," he said. "And I'll have a walkie talkie. We'll stay in touch. No problem."

Maggie stared at her parents. Neither one of them had asked what she wanted to do. Either way, one of them would be mad at her. She sighed and, still in her pajamas, slipped past her father, out the door of the camper. Outside the world was grey. There was sunlight on the mountain peaks but it hadn't yet crawled down into the valley. The dogs came, licked her face and hands. The sheep were still peacefully lying down.

The ground was cold on her bare feet. She went to the fire and poured herself a mug of coffee. She wasn't supposed to drink coffee; her mother said it was bad for her, but Maggie loved it with cream and honey. And she figured if she was old enough to work as a sheepherder, she was old enough to drink coffee.

Her father came out of the camper, looking angry, "I want to come with you, Dad," she said.

"Good," he said. "But you'll have to tell your mom. The other crew will be along pretty quick. They have a truck as well. Maybe one of them will go with your mom, keep her from worrying too much."

"Oh, great," Maggie thought. She hated feeling caught between her parents. But at least this morning, she wouldn't have to feel guilty for deserting her mother. She liked to spend time with her mother but lately she was more fascinated by the sheep, the dogs, and the things she was learning. Shine was a good teacher. She knew what the sheep should be doing. She could tell if a sheep was in trouble long before Maggie or her father noticed anything was wrong. Her ears were like little black and white antennas, always moving; her nose too, twitched and sniffed, testing the wind. Sometimes Maggie tried to imitate her, turning her head from side to side so she could hear better, taking little tiny quick sniffs through her nose, so she could smell better. She was beginning to notice more and more as she got used to being outside. She spent hours crouched on a rock, watching the sheep, listening to birds, smelling the sharp powdery smell of sun on granite, the cold scent of clouds or fog, the sharp and tangy smell of spruce trees and drying grass. She never had time to be bored. Sometimes she wondered what her friends were doing back in the valley, but usually she forgot all about them.

One day, when she was sitting there, a pica came and sat at her feet, chewing a peace of grass. Maggie sat perfectly still, hardly breathing. The pica had tiny bright black eyes, brown fur, short stubby tail. Maggie could see its heart beating under its ribs, its tiny black nose twitching.

Every day, she was learning more about the mountains, the plants and animals around her. Her parents had brought bird and plant and animal identification books with them. Around the fire, at night, they lectured her and each other, looked up the names of everything, tried to make sure they had everything properly tagged and labeled. Maggie listened; then she escaped, spent the long evenings tucked into her bunk in the camper, reading comic books, or cuddling her worn ancient elephant, dreaming about the great things she might do one day when she was a grown up and free to do what she wanted.

But this morning, another truck came growling up the logging road. They could hear it coming a long time before it arrived. By then, Jo was out of the camper, and was busy mixing up pancake batter, making more coffee, and cooking a big pan of scrambled eggs, onions, red peppers, and mushrooms.

"That's pretty much the last of our supplies, Len," she said. "No more eggs, no more flour, no more butter. I don't like being so short of food."

"Hey, don't worry so much. There'll be new supplies at Rainbow River," he said. "It's a better camp than this. There's a picnic table, a fireplace, and even a real outhouse."

The new truck stopped and an older couple got out. Rex and Shine leapt up to greet them because these were their real owners. After breakfast, Jo and the new woman, Claire, bustled around cleaning and packing. Claire was short and muscular, with grey hair and bright blue eyes.

"I'll go just ahead of you in our truck, Jo," she said. "Nothing to worry about. We do this trip every year."

Maggie, Len, and the other shepherd, Bill, went with Shine, Rex and Bill's other dog, Ben, to get the sheep moving.

"Gonna be a long long day, Maggie," Bill said. "Lots of scrambling over rocks and brush. Think you're up to it?" He seemed to be about a hundred years old. He was short with bow legs, a weathered face that looked like shoe leather, twinkling blue eyes, and a short white beard. Maggie thought he looked like Santa Claus.

"She's tough and fast and great with the sheep," boasted her father. "She'll be fine."

Bill just grunted. Ben, the new dog, was older as well. He stayed right at Bill's heels, until with a simple hand motion, Bill sent him towards the sheep at a half run, half crouch, staring at them with his bright beady brown eyes. Len sent Rex and Shine out as well.

Then whistling and shouting, they got the sheep moving in the right direction. The dogs stayed in constant motion, keeping the sheep moving, bringing up the stragglers, keeping them all gathered together. Sometimes the dogs would run to gather the sheep. Sometimes, at a whistle from Bill or Len, they would lie down, their heads on their paws, staring hard at the sheep. Their eyes seemed to say, "Don't try to get away with anything foolish."

For a while they all followed a kind of trail through the trees and over the rocks. Bill had been this way before and showed them the slashes on the trees that indicated the trail. Sometimes the sheep spread out over a steep and rocky hillside, and sometimes they were all bunched up on a narrow path that ran between giant boulders and twisted bent spruce trees. They made a lot of noise, calling to each other, the lambs baa-ing to their mothers, the mothers maa-ing back. Whenever a lamb got scared, it would run to its mother, kneel down, and have a quick drink of milk.

The sun shone hot on Maggie's back. She whistled and shouted at the sheep. They kept wanting to stop and graze. Sometimes a sheep would find itself behind a rock or a tree and lose sight of the other sheep. Then it would panic, start running back and forth, but Shine was always right there to get it moving in the right direction. Maggie laughed. Sheep were so silly.

Just before noon, they came to a large creek foaming and crashing down the hill. There was a level place on the other side of the creek, a tiny meadow full of flowers.

"We'll push them through the creek, then let them rest and graze," Bill announced. "Time for our lunch too."

The sheep were afraid of the water. It took all three of them and the dogs to get the sheep across the water and then spread out over the small meadow. Maggie was tired and wet with sweat by the time they were done. Bill made a small fire, produced some sandwiches and a teapot from his pack. Maggie's father produced more sandwiches, some juice and apples, and a couple of chocolate bars. They had a great lunch, then Bill lay back, pulled his hat over his eyes, and fell asleep. Maggie's father too, lay back and closed his eyes.

Maggie poked some more sticks into the fire, then went to sit with Shine, watching the sheep. A cold wind blew past her. She look across the meadow to the valley and the mountain peaks beyond. Clouds were drifting in, covering the distant mountains. Grey veils of rain hung between the peaks.

She went back to the fire. "Dad," she said, "Dad, there's a storm coming."

He opened his eyes, yawned and sat up. "You're right," he said. "We'd better get moving. C'mon, Bill, let's get going."

Bill was on his feet in a second and they all worked together to get the sheep moving again in the right direction. A freezing cold wind was blowing in their faces. It began to rain and the rain had teeth, tiny flakes of wet snow that clung to the grass and rocks and to Maggie's face.

They were driving the sheep down a hill that was more like a cliff, covered with humps of grassy earth, tiny rushing creeks, and rock slides. It was all slick with the snow coming down. Twice Maggie's feet slid out from under her and she fell, once hitting her bum on the rocks so hard she felt dizzy.

"Ow," she yelled. She lay there for a few minutes until the pain subsided. She was mad. Why had her father made her come on this stupid trip? She could be in the warm truck right now, reading comic books. She looked for her father but he hadn't heard her or perhaps he was too busy to pay much attention.

The snow was getting thicker. Maggie had fallen behind. She got up and limped carefully down the hill, afraid of falling again. She knew she should try to go faster but she was too afraid of falling. She was getting very cold. She had brought a light summer jacket with her, but it wasn't much protection against the icy cutting wind. She shoved her hands in her pockets but she had to keep taking them out again to hold on to bushes or bits of grass to help her on the steep slippery slope.

She stopped. "Dad," she called into the wind. "Dad, where are you?" but she couldn't hear anything. The wind and the snow muffled all sound. Miserable, she kept on trudging down the hill. She was getting madder and madder at her father. He was supposed to look after her. What would her mother say if she knew Maggie was out here in the snow, wet and freezing cold. Her feet in their light sneakers were soaking wet and turning numb. Her jeans were wet on her bum and all down one leg where she'd fallen down.

She hoped the storm would blow by quickly, like mountain storms often did. Then the sun would come out and she would be warm again.

She had lost all sight of the sheep herd, the dogs and the men. But all she had to do was keep going down the hill and she would catch up with them. Surely they would wait for her once they got to the bottom. It seemed to take forever but finally the steep slope levelled off and she saw a black shape ahead through the snow. It was a tiny round lake; the water was black and still. There were trees all around the edge, but no sign of a thousand sheep, three dogs and two men. The snow hissed as it hit the black water.

"Dad?" she called again. "Dad, where are you?" The wind had died down somewhat, but it was still snowing. She should be able to find tracks, should be able to tell which way they'd gone. She circled all the way around the lake but there was no sign anyone had ever been here.

"Dad," she screamed. "Dad, come back. Come and get me. I can't find you."

She went past the edge of the lake but there was only a jumble of boulders, with no way down. There was no path, no noisy herd of sheep. She tucked her freezing hands inside her jacket and tried to think. She must have taken a wrong turn somewhere. But where? She'd have to climb back up the hill, and try and find where they went.

"Dad," she said, and felt two tears start in her eyes. She was so cold. What was she going to do? She was lost in the snow, in the mountains.

Chapter Four

Suddenly, a black shape appeared above her, running towards her. She opened her mouth to scream, and the tiny black and white furry body appeared in the snow, nose to the ground, trailing her.

"Shine," she said. "Oh, Shine, good girl." She dropped to her knees and hugged the dog, who wiggled all over and wrinkled up her lips in her happy dog snarl-grin.

"C'mon, girl, let's find Dad," Maggie said. Together, they climbed back up the slope. When Maggie stopped, uncertain of which way to go, Shine nudged her from behind as if she were a silly sheep.

"Okay, okay," she said crossly. "I'm going." It took quite a while to climb back up the slope and find the place where they had turned off to go along the hill but soon she could hear the unmistakable sounds of the sheep, and smell smoke from a fire. Her father and Bill had a small fire burning inside a shelter formed by two huge boulders.

"Maggie!" he said. "I was worried sick about you. I thought you were right behind me, but then we got this far, and I couldn't see you. I thought you must be coming along right behind us. I was just going back to look for you. Then Shine took off. I hoped she could probably find you better than I could. What a great little dog. You're all wet, honey. Come and get warm."

He gave her a quick hug. His face looked worried. "Bill's hurt his leg," he said. "That's why I didn't come looking for you right away. I had to get a fire going, which wasn't easy in this snow. I didn't know what to do first, look for you or look after Bill. But at least you're okay." He sighed heavily as he led the way back to the fire.

"We're in a real jam here," he said. "I don't know how we're going to manage. We can't stay here. We're not equipped to stay over night. We've got to get the sheep to shelter and Bill's the only one who knows the way."

Bill was sitting on the ground holding his leg.

"Twisted my ankle again," he said, shaking his head. "Old fool that I am. I've done it before. Every time it gets worse. I can walk on it but it's going to be

30

slow and I'll have to lean on a stick and take my time. Len, Maggie, you'll have to work the sheep without me."

Maggie crouched by the fire, shivering. She didn't want to go anywhere, especially not back into the wall of white swirling around them.

"Maggie's just a little girl," Len said. "And she's had a heck of a scare. It's too much to ask her to help herd. She can stay back and make sure you're okay. Maggie, honey, I'm sorry. I shouldn't have brought you along. I knew it could be dangerous but I never thought anything would happen on such a sunny day. Your mom is going to be so mad at me for not making sure you stayed safe the truck."

"I'm freezing," Maggie said angrily, her teeth chattering. "I want to go home." She felt tears in her eyes but she held them back. Her throat hurt. She wanted her mom.

"Right! Just what I'm trying to figure out how to do."

"No, I mean, to our real home. Back to the farm. I want to see my friends. I want to have fun. I hate it here. I HATE these stupid mountains." Maggie began to cry. She didn't really want to and she knew her father had enough to deal with but she was too cold and tired to hold it back.

"Maggie!" her dad exploded. "Get it together. We've got to help each other out of this. I told you we're in a jam. Now you listen. No more whining. We can't deal with it right now. You help Bill, and I'll deal with the sheep. Thank God for the dogs. I'd never

31

manage without them. Now let's get going. We don't have much time before it starts to get dark."

"Guess we don't have much choice," Bill said. "I like your spirit, Len. Okay, you're the trail boss on this move. All you have to do is keep the sheep moving. From here on, there's a trail, and the dogs know the way. They did this trek with me last year. But you've got to keep the stragglers moving and keep the strays from getting lost. Maggie and I will be right behind you. We've got to go as fast as we can or we'll be trying to move this herd in the dark, which is just too risky on these steep hills. Okay, upsy-daisy." He hoisted himself to his feet with a grunt of pain and leaned on Len's shoulder.

"It hurts but I'll manage," he grinned.

The next few hours were a nightmare for Maggie. It had stopped snowing but a cold wind blew right through her wet clothes. She concentrated on putting one foot in front of the other. She didn't want to fall down again. She kept her hands wrapped together under her coat. She kept thinking of her mother. Sometimes she thought of what she would like to eat when she made it back to the camper. She tried to lose herself in a daydream but nothing worked. She was furious with her father. He didn't even come back to check and make sure she was okay.

Bill limped along the trail in front of her. Sometimes he turned around to peer at her and see if she was okay. From far away, she could hear the baa-ing of the sheep and an occasional shout from her father. Shine kept circling back to check on her. Finally, just as dusk was deepening and blue shadows were growing in all the hollows, she saw lights far below on the mountain.

"There it is. There's the camp," her father yelled. "Fantastic. Hot supper, here we come."

Jo and Claire heard the noise of the sheep coming and came to meet them with flashlights and a thermos of hot coffee. Claire gasped when she saw Bill limping.

"Oh, Bill," she said. "Your poor ankle, again." Claire and Jo got on either side of him to help him down the hill.

"Maggie," said Jo. "Oh, Len. Maggie's half frozen. Come on, honey, let's get you inside."

Maggie went slowly down the hill. Her feet were far away, lead weights she lifted up on the bottom of each heavy leg. Finally, she crawled into the warm camper, shut the door, bent over to take off her shoes. The knots were twisted tight and her fingers were too numb to undo them. She managed to slide them off, then peeled off her wet socks, jeans and jacket and crawled into her sleeping bag.

From far away, she heard her mother's voice. "Here, Maggie, drink some hot soup."

The soup was hot, thick, and absolutely delicious. When she had finished it, she lay back down and closed her eyes. Swirling mist and black rocks and endless cliffs filled her vision. She heard the door open again and a wet nose nudged her cheek.

"Shine," she said. "C'mon girl." Shine's black furry body wedged itself beside Maggie on the narrow bunk. Her plume-like tail thumped frantically. Then having made sure Maggie was all right, she went to the camper door, pushed it open, and went back outside.

"Good girl," whispered Maggie drowsily. "You looked after all of us today." She could hear her mother and father talking outside. The kerosene heater sent a blast of heat towards her but she couldn't stop shivering. She wrapped the sleeping bag tightly around her shoulders. She was too tired, she thought, to even make up a story to put herself to sleep.

When she closed her eyes, all she could see were images of swirling snow, black cliffs, the endless white humped backs of the sheep going along ahead of her. The mountains had sent her a challenge, a real one, not a daydream. She knew she had passed an important test of some kind, even though she wasn't sure what it was, or just what it meant.

Chapter Five

"Len, we need to talk," said Maggie's mother. "We need a family meeting." She looked very serious. Maggie was sitting across the fire from her. It was the next day, early morning and she was drinking coffee with cream and honey and eating her favourite food, toast covered with thick homemade raspberry jam. Her feet and legs still hurt from the long hard journey over the mountains. She sighed. Her parents were so big on family meetings but Maggie could never see how they really solved anything.

Claire and Bill had packed up and gone and Maggie's family were alone again with the sheep, the dogs, and a new, beautiful mountain valley to explore.

"Maggie had a close call yesterday. Too close. I'm not very happy with the way things are going this summer," Jo continued." We need to talk this over."

Maggie's father nodded. "I'm sorry, Jo," he said. "I didn't think it would be that dangerous. But it came out all right. Maggie was great. She helped out with Bill and the sheep."

"That's not the point, Len. She was in danger. She shouldn't have been there at all. She should have been safe and warm in the truck with me."

Maggie's father nodded again. "You're right," he said. "I didn't realise how easy it would be for her to get lost. We all learned a lot. It was a good lesson in how careful we have to be up here. But Maggie learned a good lesson as well."

"And another thing...I want to work with the sheep, too, not just be stuck in camp cooking and driving the truck. I know as much as you do. Maybe some days you can stay in camp and do the cleaning and cooking and Maggie and I can spend the day with the sheep." Jo's face was pink and she looked very determined.

"Okay," he said, "okay, Jo. You're right. I guess I've been kind of selfish." He looked so miserable Maggie almost burst out laughing.

"And no more taking chances with Maggie. She's to stick closer to camp. Maggie, I want to know where you are at all times, no more wandering off. I've been so busy getting the camp organised and making us a home in the wilderness, I haven't paid enough attention to you, but now we're settled again, that's going to change. It's too dangerous up here to have you running around on your own. You stay with either your dad or me."

Maggie sat between them poking at the fire with her stick. Words ran around in her head like little black bugs. Her parents were so big on talking over things and having "family meetings" but somehow they always did most of the talking. She tried to think what it was that she wanted to say. She felt confused. She wanted to say that none of this was her idea. She wanted to tell them how much she missed hanging around with her friends, watching TV and eating ice cream but that wasn't really true anymore. She had discovered that the mountains were huge, scary, but exciting. She wanted to yell at her stupid parents that they never listened to her, that they didn't care about her but that wasn't really true either. She didn't know what she felt. She opened her mouth. Nothing came out. Her parents looked expectantly at her..

"I'm going to check on the sheep," she mumbled, and ran out of the camp. Her parents stared after her. She whistled to the dogs as she left, and Shine came running, wriggling her body and jumping up and down to show her happiness at seeing Maggie. Behind her, Maggie heard her mother call her name. She pretended not to hear.

"C'mon, Shine," Maggie said. Shine ran and grabbed a stick and tossed it in the air and then looked at Maggie. Her tongue lolled out of her mouth. "I

37

don't feel like playing, Shine," Maggie said. "I feel horrible." Shine came and stayed at her side and stared up at her like she was trying to understand. Maggie wondered what life would be like if Shine were her dog. At the end of summer, Maggie and her parents would go home and Shine and Rex would go back to Bill and Claire.

The morning sun was hot, glistening on the rocks, grass and flowers. Picas and marmots whistled from the rocks. Tiny foaming waterfalls ran down over the smooth granite cliffs surrounding the valley. The sheep were spread out over the valley, eating the lush grass. There were piles of stumps and branches left over from logging. Tiny trees poked their heads through the grass. Maggie found a great place to sit, on a high rock looking over the whole valley. Her parents would be mad at her for walking away when they were talking.

She wondered how to tell them she didn't want to talk, she wanted to sit here with Shine, the sun hot on her back, dreaming and thinking about things. Suddenly, there was a commotion on the far edge of the sheep herd. Shine took off like a little black bullet, barking ferociously. Maggie followed, wondering what was going on. Sheep were running towards her. Something was scaring them. Then something huge and brown came out from behind a lump of trees. Maggie slid to a halt, her heart thumping wildly. The huge brown animal was a bear, and, from what her father had told her, it was probably a grizzly bear.

The dogs barked furiously. The bear stopped and looked at them, swinging his huge head from side to side. Maggie stared for a moment, then turned and ran as fast as her legs could go, back towards the camp. Halfway there, she met her mother and father, running towards her.

"A bear," she gasped. "A big, brown bear. Over there. By the sheep."

Her parents looked at each other.

"The dogs," Maggie went on. "The dogs are chasing it. Don't let it hurt them."

"That bear won't lay a paw on the dogs," said her father gently. "They know what they're doing. Remember, they've done this job before. They'll probably drive it away but I'd better go check."

Her mom put an arm around Maggie's shoulder. "Why, honey, you're shaking," she said. "Don't be scared. The bear won't come over here. Remember,

40

we're in his territory. We've invaded his home. He's probably trying to figure it out. But bears hate people and noise. He'll go away. The dogs and your dad won't take any chances. They'll stay far away and just watch until the bear leaves."

"But Mom, they could get hurt."

"They'll be very careful," her mom assured her. "Your father knows what he's doing."

"Oh, sure," said Maggie. "Like he did yesterday. He didn't even come and look for me. He didn't even care that I was lost."

"What do you mean?" said her mother. "He said you got a little behind and Shine went to find you."

"I was lost," Maggie said. "I was lost and freezing and nobody came. I called and called. Only Shine came."

"Oh, Maggie," said her mom. "We didn't know. No one did. Shine is a great dog. We owe her a debt. But if your dad had known you were lost, he would have done everything he could to find you."

"Mom, do you like it here? I mean, it's so different from home."

Her mom looked at her. "I know everything is strange for you. I know you probably miss your friends. But yes, I love it here. And you've learned so much. You've been a big help already. Yesterday, you were very brave. We're proud of you."

Maggie sighed. "That bear was really huge," she said. "I wasn't brave. I was scared. I couldn't even think what to do."

"Honey, you are brave, and we are proud of you. And I'm scared of bears too. Really scared. C'mon, let's go make some hot chocolate and wait for your dad."

Together they went back to the camper. Maggie's father came back a little while later.

"The bear has gone," he reported. "The dogs drove it off for now. But from now on, we lock up all food in the camper at all times, and no wandering off. Maggie, no more running off like you did this morning. That was very irresponsible of you, to run away when we were trying to talk to you."

"Just look at Shine," her mother said. "She works so hard, always takes orders, pays attention. She's a huge help around here. You could learn a lot from her, Maggie. In the meantime, you're grounded for the day. You can clean up the camper. It needs it."

Maggie felt confused. One minute they were telling her she was brave, and the next they were punishing her. It didn't make any sense. She was the one who had gotten lost and cold. Now she had almost gotten eaten by a bear. Why were her parents treating her like she had done something wrong. She was mad. She hadn't expected to be grounded. What a drag. Plus, she hadn't made all of the mess in the camper and she didn't feel like cleaning anything. She went and lay down inside. She lay there all morning, reading some silly old comic books. Outside the sun shone, the wind blew through the trees, and the world went on its way. As she lay there, her mood got blacker. Her parents didn't understand her. They

42

hadn't asked what she was upset about or why she had run off. She had actually been acting as the responsible one, going to check on the sheep when her parents were wasting time arguing.

All they ever did was order her around. She was lonesome. She wanted to lay on the beach for a whole day and do nothing. How would her parents like that? They were treating her like a baby, thinking she couldn't even take care of herself, when the day before she had helped to handle a whole herd of thousand foolish, confused and frightened sheep; she had been lost in the mountains, and she had found her own way back to the camp, her and Shine.

Finally, her growling stomach drove her out of the camper. The fire was still smouldering but neither of her parents was in sight. She was afraid to go and look for them. What if she ran into the bear? She sat by the fire, feeling more and more lonesome and hungry. Finally, she made herself a sandwich, and poured herself a glass of lemonade.

Then she went and lay down in the camper and fell asleep. When she woke up, she was feeling much better. She heard her mother and father's voices outside. When she went outside and stood by the fire, yawning, she saw it was already evening.

Her mother handed her a bowl of stew, a big glass of milk, and a hot biscuit slathered with butter and honey.

"Are you feeling better, Maggie?" her mother asked. "I had a great afternoon with your father, looking after the sheep. I came to check on you a couple of times but you were asleep. You must have been exhausted. Just look at that sunset. It's so beautiful here, isn't it?"

Maggie nodded through a mouthful of food.

"Your father and I are very proud of how hard you work, and how much you have learned." Her mom went on. "We should have told you that this morning, and then you wouldn't have been upset."

"That wasn't it!" Maggie said. The words came bursting out and surprised even her. "You and Dad don't listen to me. I never get a chance to talk. I'm growing up, you know. I'm eleven now, remember. I'm not a baby anymore. You never listen to me. You always say we're a team, but I'm just a kid. How can I be part of the team? You say let's talk and then we have family discussions and I don't get to say anything. If I try, you just tell me I'm being disrespectful. I never wanted to come here. I wanted to stay home all summer. I was scared to tell you I wanted to go home. Because I thought you wouldn't listen. You never ever listen!"

There was a long silence when she finished. Len and Jo looked at each other and then at the ground.

"Maybe you've got a point," her mother said. "Maybe we could work out some way for you to go home. It's pretty dangerous here." Maggie's heart lurched. "You'd have to stay with Auntie Robin." Maggie groaned. She hated staying at Auntie Robin's.

Her house was always perfectly neat. Maggie couldn't do anything there without permission. She couldn't eat a cookie or ride her bike or even watch television.

"No way," she said. "Besides, I wasn't finished. What I wanted to say is, it's pretty cool here. I like it. You guys were smart to think of this. I just don't want to be treated like a baby. If I'm part of the team, then you have to treat me that way."

Jo came over and put her arm around Maggie. "I'm sorry if you think we don't listen. But you have to learn to tell us what you want. You father and I can't read your mind. We'll all try and do better, okay?"

Maggie leaned against her mother and hugged her back. Her mom smelt so good and she was so soft and warm. Maggie was suddenly sorry she had been so mad at her parents. They really tried to be good parents. They just didn't get stuff most of the time. She figured they couldn't help getting mixed up.

"We knew you'd just love a summer in the mountains, away from that stupid television, out here in the middle of Mother Nature. We knew you'd learn so much," her father said. Maggie sighed. Her father was never going to get it.

"I still like television too," she muttered. There was another silence.

"We should work out a schedule of who gets to look after the sheep," Maggie's mother said. "You can help in the camp, too, Len. Sometimes you and Maggie can take turns cooking, cleaning up and looking after the fire."

"That's a very very good idea," Len said enthusiastically. "I think you're right. I think we'll do that. We can all share the work here and we can all look after each other. We can all have a great summer together. We're going to be a real team after all."

Maggie just shook her head. Parental units were so dependable. They never changed.

Chapter Six

Maggie stopped, and held her side. She was breathing hard.

"Wait, Shine," she called. "That'll do. Here to me." Obediently Shine came and lay down at her feet. Her eyes, however, never left the sheep she and Maggie had been moving and her small muscular body still quivered with eagerness.

"That was great," her father said, emerging from a clump of trees where he'd been watching their progress. "You've really caught on to the shepherd business. You and Shine work well together. We'll have to figure out some way for you both to visit when we head down the mountain."

The summer was going so fast, Maggie thought, as she caught her breath. They had already been here over a month. Less than one more month to go. Her mother and father had been showing her all the things they learned at sheepherding school. They praised her to the skies, too much praise, Maggie thought. Ever since her outburst, they had treated her very carefully, asking her opinion about everything, including her in every decision they made. Sometimes Maggie wished they would just relax. But then they'd always been like that. They cared about everything, it seemed, the environment, pollution, everybody's health. They were always taking icky vitamins and worrying about what to eat. There was too much stuff in the world to worry about, Maggie thought. She just wanted to have a good time.

Working the sheep with Shine had proven to be a lot more fun than she'd expected. But in a few more short weeks the summer would be over. Then she and her mother would drive the camper back down the mountain to their own house. Maggie's father would stay behind and someone else would come to help look after the sheep. They would stay in the mountains until fall, and then the sheep would have to be driven down the mountain to their new home. Shine and Rex would go back home.

But Maggie didn't know how she was going to say goodbye to Shine. She realised as long as Shine was around, she felt safe. Shine's bright eyes and quick ears let her know if there were any wild animals around. Maggie had learned to watch Shine carefully. If Shine put her nose up, sniffed the wind and growled, Maggie knew something scary was prowling around. She hadn't seen the bear again, but several times, the dogs had taken off, barking, and she had heard something heavy crashing through the brush. Shine always stayed close to her when they were wandering around in the bush. Maggie knew Shine would protect her from anything dangerous.

"That bear is still around," her father had announced the night before. "I've seen his tracks. But he's smart, and not taking any chances. He doesn't like the dogs. We probably won't see him again. But we should still be careful and not wander off too far."

Maggie's mother made sure they burned all their scraps from dinner, locked all the food in the camper, and kept everything very clean.

One night, Maggie had asked her parents if they could keep Shine after the summer.

"Can't we buy her?" Maggie asked. "We could keep her for ourselves and then, next summer, we can go sheepherding again."

Her parents looked at each other and frowned. "Maggie," said her father, "Shine is a working dog. She loves her work. She takes a lot of pride in it, just like you do, like we all do. She'd be bored on the farm. Border collies don't make good pets. They get upset without a job to do."

"We could find her a job," Maggie argued. "We could get some sheep or something. And she's a good watchdog."

"Maggie, Shine is worth a lot of money," her mother said. "More than we can afford. And you're right. We need a watchdog. We'll get you a puppy. You could train it. Wouldn't you like that? We'll get you a nice golden retriever."

Maggie liked the idea of a new puppy, but she hadn't given up on the idea of keeping Shine. Surely there was some way. And she was sure Shine would miss her too.

After their sheepherding practice, she and Shine went to sit side by side on their favourite place, a high rock overlooking the meadow where the sheep were grazing. The sheep were spread out all over the wide alpine meadow. The sun was very hot. It had been very hot and dry for two weeks now.

That afternoon, Maggie and her mom went swimming in the little lake in the middle of the valley. Despite the heat, the water was ice cold.

"It's like ice," Maggie squealed as she waded slowly into the shallow blue pool.

"That's almost what it is," said her mother. "There's still snow above us on the peaks. That's what we're swimming in, melted snow." After jumping in the freezing water, Maggie and her mother lay on the grass and toasted themselves in the hot sun. Maggie's skin was tanned very brown and her long brown hair had blond streaks in it from the sun.

Maggie heard a low rumble in the distance. She looked up. Although the sky was still blue, a heavy purple-black cloud was hanging in a cleft between the mountains. An occasional distant rumble came from it. It was far away and didn't seem too frightening.

50

But by late afternoon, the clouds had built into towering walls.

While Maggie and her parents ate supper, a wind came up and soon black clouds were blotting out the whole sky.

"Looks like we're in for quite a storm," said Maggie's father. "Maggie, you come with me and we'll get the sheep bedded down early. They're going to be nervous and hard to manage. We have to keep them away from any tall trees. Lightning likes tall trees."

While they were on their way to collect the sheep, a fork of lightning lanced down and hit the nearest mountain peak. Thunder boomed and echoed through the whole valley.

Maggie jumped. She was used to lightning storms. During the summers, on the farm, at the end of a very hot day, sometimes a lightning storm would light up the valley. Maggie remembered one storm where her father had taken her outside and explained to her that the lightning was really electricity, like the light in lightbulbs and the spark in electric cords. He told her that lightning wouldn't hurt her, that it almost always hit the tops of mountains, and then he showed her that their house was protected by a lightning rod. After that she felt safe during storms.

But now the sky, with the lightning in it, seemed right above her head. The clouds were like an inky black ceiling. By the time they got the sheep settled down on a clear patch of earth, the wind was whipping and roaring through the trees. Maggie tried hard not to be scared but she wanted to run back to the camper, crawl into her warm bunk, and put her pillow over her head. Shine was nervous too. She whimpered and stayed close to Maggie.

"Maggie, you go back to the camp," her father said. "I'll stay here with the dogs. Tell your mom to leave the coffee on. I'm going to have to stay awake until this storm is over."

Maggie made her way back to the camper, jumping every time another fork of lightning sizzled down from the sky. She stayed away from any tall trees. Her mother was nervous too. She was just putting the last of the food inside the camper.

"Oh, Maggie, I'm so glad you're back," she said. "The lightning is so close. Where's your Dad?"

"He said he's going to stay out until the storm is over. He said to keep the coffee hot."

At that moment, another lightning bolt sizzled down from the sky, followed by thunder so loud they both jumped and Maggie gave a little terrified yelp.

"C'mon," said her mother. "Inside. This is too scary. We'll close the curtains and read to each other, and pretend we're home and safe. Oh dear, I hope your father is okay. That lightning is too close. I sure hope it doesn't start any fires."

"Fires!" Maggie thought. "Oh, no." Her stomach turned over.

She followed her mother into the camper. They closed the curtains and Maggie's mother got out a

52

magazine and Maggie got one of her favourite books, *Lassie Come Home,* and they lay down side by side in one of the bunks and tried to read.

But outside the thunder was getting louder and more frequent. The wind was so strong it was rocking the camper. Maggie's mother pulled back the curtain and gave a little scream.

"Fire!" she yelped "Oh, no! Look, lightning has started a fire on the side of the mountain. Oh, Maggie, I've got to go check on your father. I've got to make sure he's okay."

Maggie could see a giant tree blazing like an enormous torch, on the far side of the valley. Her mother put on a jacket and tied a scarf over her hair.

"I'll be right back," she said. "Maggie, you stay here. Don't go outside."

"Mom," Maggie said, "shouldn't we stay here until Dad comes?"

"No, no," said her mother. "I've got to make sure he's okay. What if he needs help? You just wait right here."

"I'm coming too," Maggie said.

"No," her mother said. "It's too dangerous. The lightning is too close. Stay here."

She went outside and the door of the camper slammed behind her.

Maggie curled up on her own bunk. Her legs were shaking and she was shivering. She wrapped herself in a blanket and closed her eyes, trying to keep out the sights and sounds of the storm but that didn't help. It only made things scarier. She sat up and knelt on the bunk and looked out the window. The tree was still burning and now some other trees around it were burning too. She kept the blanket wrapped tight, as if it could make her feel better.

But at that moment, Maggie heard the patter of rain on the camper. The patter quickly turned into a roar. It sounded like a waterfall coming down on the roof. The fire disappeared.

Suddenly she heard voices and laughter. The camper door opened and both her parents came in. They were soaking wet and breathless from running.

"Maggie, my dear," her father laughed. "You can come out of your blanket cave. The storm is over. This rain should take care of any fires. Whew, where's that coffee, Jo. I'm soaked." Her mother lit the small propane stove in the camper and put the coffee on to heat. Then she got out dry clothes for both of them.

"Is everything okay?" said Maggie. "Where are the dogs?"

"They're still out with the sheep," her mother said. "Shine wanted to come and check on you but I made her stay behind. The funny thing is, she's such a brave dog but she's afraid of lightning. She kept whimpering and she wanted to come back to the camper so bad. I actually had to order her to stay. You know, you're right, Maggie. I think she has decided she is your dog. She seems to want to be around you all the time."

Maggie finally went to sleep, after they all had hot chocolate made with cream and marshmallows. Her heart was singing. This time she made up a dream of going to the beach with Shine and her friends. They would be so impressed when she showed them what Shine could do. She and Shine belonged together. She was becoming more and more sure of that.

Chapter Seven

Maggie woke from a deep sleep, feeling groggy. From far away, she could hear the dogs barking. Then she heard her father's feet thump onto the floor of the camper. "Now what?" she thought. After the excitement of the storm, the last couple of weeks had been very peaceful.

"What's going on?" she said.

"I don't know," he said. "Something is after the sheep. Wait here." He went outside and Maggie heard him running away from the camper. She looked out the window. It was dawn. The sky was a faint pink.

The dark was just beginning to fade away. She waited, sitting up in bed, the covers wrapped around her knees.

"What if Dad needs me?" she thought. She jumped out of bed, pulled on a T-shirt, overalls and sneakers, then wrapped a blanket around her shoulders. Her mother had gone back to sleep.

Suddenly the camper door opened. Len dashed in. His face was white. "A cougar," he gasped. "It's up a tree. The dogs have treed it."

He yanked open a cupboard door and pulled out a rifle.

" Are you going to shoot it?" Maggie said.

"I have to," he said. "It killed two sheep and now the dogs have it up a tree. I'm afraid it will jump down and hurt the dogs. Darn, I hate killing anything." His voice was shaking.

He ran out of the trailer. Maggie grabbed a jacket and followed. After all, he hadn't told her to stay behind. It was cold outside the camper. The dogs were still barking. Maggie's father was running and she ran behind him. He didn't seem to notice she was there.

When they came up to the tree where the dogs were, Maggie looked up at the tree. It wasn't very tall. The dogs were jumping up against the tree trunk, barking and growling. Maggie couldn't see anything. The tree branches were too thick. She came closer.

Suddenly, her father yelled. "Look out," he said. "Shine, Rex, come here." Now Maggie could hear another sound, a loud hissing snarling sound. A yellow shape was coming down the tree. The dogs and Len were running back from the tree. The cougar made a huge leap, and began running, right towards Maggie. She screamed.

"Maggie!" her father yelled. "Watch out!"

Maggie stood paralysed. Suddenly a black and white shape shot between her and the cougar. There was a whirling snarling ball of yellow and black and white, and then the cougar shot off into the forest and was gone.

"Shine," yelled Maggie. She ran towards the little dog lying on the ground.

"Maggie," said her father. "Are you okay? What happened? It all happened so fast. I didn't have time to think about shooting. I was afraid I might hurt you or the dogs."

"It's Shine," Maggie yelled. "She saved me, and now she's hurt."

She knelt down beside the little dog. Shine lifted her head and licked Maggie's hand. Len knelt beside her, and felt over the dog with his hands.

"She's got a bad cut down her ribs and another on her neck," he said, "but I think she's okay. I can't find anything else. We'd better get her back to the camper so we can check her all over."

"She saved me," said Maggie. "She saw the cougar coming towards me and she ran between me and the cougar."

"She's one brave little dog," said her father. He lifted Shine in his arms and together they hurried towards the camper. Maggie's mother was waiting in the doorway. They laid Shine on the bunk and checked her carefully. The long slash down her side looked like it had been cut with a knife. Shine closed her eyes. She was panting like she had been in a long race.

"We're going to have to bandage that cut," Maggie's mother said. "But I'm afraid it might get infected. Cat bites infect so easily. She's got to get to the vet for antibiotics. Len, you'll have to take her down the mountain. Right now, you'll have to help hold her still, Maggie, while I clean and bandage that wound."

Maggie was glad her mother had taken a first aid course to get ready for their summer in the mountains. Maggie held Shine's head while her mother cleaned, disinfected and bandaged the cut. Shine never made a sound. Occasionally, she licked Maggie's hand. When she was finished, Maggie's mother wrapped a bandage all the way around Shine's body. Then she lifted her down onto a blanket on the floor. Shine looked so funny that Maggie couldn't help laughing. Shine lifted her head, sniffed the bandage, then lay back down again.

From far away, they could hear the sheep bawling. Shine lifted her head, her eyes flashing. She looked anxiously at Maggie and whimpered.

"Look at her," said Maggie's father.

"Even hurt as she is, she wants to get back to work. She's worried about the sheep. What a great little dog." He knelt and patted her head.

"Will the cougar come back, Dad?" Maggie asked.

"I don't think so," her father said. "Cougars are actually very timid. They don't usually attack when there are people or dogs around. I think that cougar was as terrified as we were. It's probably still running. But Maggie, you sure scared me. I didn't know you were there. When I saw the cougar run towards you, my heart almost stopped."

"Me too," said Maggie. "I was too scared to move."

"But not Shine," said Maggie's mother. "She's the smart one. She knew what to do. We owe her a big thank you!"

Shine whimpered and scratched at the blanket. "Okay, girl," said Len. "I'll go check on everything. Then Rex and I will come back and have some breakfast before I take off. This is a heck of a way to start the morning and I'm hungry!"

He disappeared out the door. Maggie was tired. She went and lay down on her bed but she couldn't sleep. She kept seeing the bright yellow coat of the cougar as it bounded towards her. Would the cougar have hurt her? She was more determined than ever now to keep Shine. How could her parents let Shine go? What could she say to change their minds.

"Maggie, come and get your breakfast," said her mother. "I made you your favourite, hot chocolate and toast with jam. I'm so nervous I can't relax. I keep waiting for your father to come back. I keep thinking I hear things."

"Mom, Shine saved my life," said Maggie. "We have to keep her."

Her mother laughed. "Maggie, you are just as stubborn and determined as Shine. You two are so much alike. But you have to think about what Shine wants too. Working with sheep is her life. You saw how determined she was to get back to work. We have to think this over very carefully and try and make the right decision. Now come eat your breakfast. Later, when you're father gets back from town, we'll talk the whole matter over as a family."

Her father came back to the camp. "Everything's fine," he said. "Maggie, you're in charge for the day while I get our brave little dog here to the vet." And he lifted Shine in his arms, got into the truck, and drove away.

Chapter Eight

Maggie wandered unhappily through on trees on her way to favourite lookout. Shine limped beside her. Tomorrow, she and her mother would finish packing up the camper and then they would drive the pickup back down the long winding mountain road to their farm. Maggie's father had gone with the sheep over the mountains to yet another valley. Just before he left, they had all stood in front of the camper while Maggie's dad arranged the camera on a stump so it would take another picture of them all.

Another border collie had come with another shepherd to help move the sheep. Shine was off duty. She was supposed to take it easy until she finished healing. She was still limping but she wanted to get back to work.

Maggie wondered what it would like to be home again. She felt so much different, older, and smarter. She would have many adventures to tell about but now her quiet life at home seemed boring. The idea of going back to school, sitting in a classroom all winter seemed impossible after the freedom of the high mountain peaks and all her adventures. She hadn't wanted to come and now she couldn't stand to leave.

"Why is life so weird, Shine? I'm not ready for summer to be over. I thought I would hate it here and be so glad to get home but I'm not," Maggie said out loud. "And what if you have to go away? Then what will I do?"

Shine pricked up her ears and wagged her tail. She loved exploring the woods with Maggie, and Maggie always felt safe with Shine beside her. Maggie and Shine came to the lookout, sat down and looked around. All summer Maggie had been looking at the mountains around her and longing to explore farther and farther. Today, she had packed a lunch, some matches and jacket in a small backpack. She had begged her mother for permission to go on a picnic as far as the lookout, and finally her mother agreed as long as she didn't go any farther and she kept Shine beside her.

Maggie stared and stared at the mountain in front of her. Her father had told her it was called Haystack Mountain. He had been saying all summer that he'd sure like to try to climb it if he had more time. It didn't look that high. Because they were already on top of the mountains, the peaks here were more like small hills. Suddenly, she made up her mind. "Come on, Shine," she said. "We can at least give it a try."

Maggie and Shine waded through an icy creek, went through a forest of small twisted spruce trees, and crossed a swampy area where mosquitoes whined around their faces. Finally they came to the base of the mountain. Haystack Mountain stuck up into the sky like a jagged tooth. At its base was a jumble of broken rocks that Maggie's father said was called talus.

Maggie picked her way from rock to rock, climbing steadily upwards. Finally the talus slope ended and she found a ridge of rock and small trees that she could follow towards the peak. A warm wind whipped her hair around her ears. As she climbed higher and higher, she found she could see far over the mountains, over into the next valley and far far away to where a lake lay in blue shadows. Somewhere beside that lake was their farm, their white farmhouse, Maggie's room with its worn carpet and familiar patchwork quilt.

Maggie climbed and climbed. Shine stayed beside her. Finally, she came to a place where the ridge she was following narrowed to path only a foot wide. The

64

rock on either side dropped off to a steep cliff hundreds of feet high. Maggie stopped. She looked at the ridge. The empty air on either side made her stomach feel hollow.

"If it was on the ground, you could walk it easy," she said to herself. She waited, taking deep breaths until the shaky hollow feeling went away. She studied the ridge carefully. There were rocks and small trees she could hang onto. Finally, she stepped out slowly on the narrow path. Shine followed just as slowly and carefully behind. Step by step, together they crossed the narrow ridge to a jumble of large boulders. There, just beyond, was the summit.

There was a triangular pile of rocks on the summit and a small book in a plastic bag. Inside the book was a list of names and dates. Maggie added her and Shine's names, then she sat on the ground, staring at the view. Suddenly she heard a piercing whistle. An eagle was hanging in the sky, staring at her. Maggie laughed and waved. "It's okay," she called. "We're just leaving."

It was getting late. Blue shadows were creeping over the mountains. Carefully, they went back down the ridge. When she came to the narrow part, she realised she couldn't see the handholds very clearly. The darkness was stealing her confidence. She began to step out onto the narrow part and then stopped. Her stomach turned and twisted. She glanced at the huge empty space on either side of the ridge and sat down, suddenly dizzy, hanging on to the solid rock beneath her. She hadn't realised it was so late. Her mother would be really worried.

"Shine," she said. Her voice sounded weak and whining even in her own ears. "Shine, what am I going to do? I'm scared."

Shine came back and licked Maggie's face. Maggie held on to the warm muscular body of the little dog. "Aren't you ever afraid, Shine?" she asked. Shine stared intently into Maggie's eyes. Then she took a step towards the ridge and looked back at Maggie to see if she were coming.

"Okay, Shine. I know. I have to do it." Maggie took a deep breath and closed her eyes. From somewhere inside her, a quiet trickle of strength began to drown out the shouting voices of the fear.

"One step at a time," she thought to herself. "I won't look down. I'll just go one step at a time. I won't fall. It's up to me to decide and I won't fall."

She opened her eyes. It was even darker now. She stood up. Step by step, she inched her way along the knife-edged ridge. A wind came and blew her hair around her face. Shine stayed a few steps in front of her. Together, they crossed the ridge to wider ground.

They flew down as quick as they could over the wider ridge. Shine jumped from rock to rock and Maggie followed her. Her heart was singing. She had done it. She had climbed the mountain all by herself. She had conquered her fear and now she felt as light

and happy as an eagle, as if she had grown huge
wings herself and could fly down the mountain.

It was almost dark when she trudged, exhausted
into the campsite. Her legs felt like rubber from all the
climbing. She slumped into a camp chair and yawned.

"Maggie!" exclaimed her mother. "I was so worried. You were gone so long! What on earth did you think you were doing? Where did you go? You know you're not supposed to wander off. And your father isn't here to help out. I was afraid to leave the camp to look for you!"

"I'm really sorry, Mom. Shine and I went exploring and lost track of the time," said Maggie. "We did some climbing around and then we sat and stared at the view. Gosh, Mom, I thought I would be so glad to go home, but I don't know, I'm sure going to miss it here. We saw an eagle."

"Well, it is beautiful," said her mother, "but I will be very glad to get back to hot running water, showers, a washer and dryer, and my own warm soft bed. And what about school? Don't you want to see your friends? What about Ben and Brad? When we first came here, all you wanted to do was go home."

"I know," said Maggie. "But now everything seems different. Mom, what about Shine? I can't even think about not having her around. She's my best friend. If we owned her, I could keep practicing being a shepherd. I read in that magazine you guys get about sheepherding that you can even go in contests. I bet Shine and I could do really well. I bet we could win!"

"I don't know," said her mother. "I don't know what to do. Your father and I haven't been able to make a decision. Bill wants a lot of money for her. She's a valuable dog. But she may always be a little

68

stiff from her injury, so perhaps we could buy her for less. But your father thinks we can't afford it. He thinks she would be bored at the farm."

"I could get a job," said Maggie. "I could help pay for her."

"Oh, Maggie," said her mother. "You're too young to get a job."

"I've been working hard all summer," Maggie said. "I've helped with the sheep I've even helped with cooking and all that stuff. I've learned tons. I thought you said I was part of the team." She turned her head so her mother wouldn't see the tears in her eyes. "Next summer, I'll know what to do. Then we'll really be a team."

"But Maggie, I thought you hated it here. Remember when you said you were so bored, and all you wanted to do was go home?"

"Oh, Mom," said Maggie, with exasperation. "That was ages ago. Everything is different now." Jeez, didn't her mother notice anything?

"Well, maybe you're right," said her mother. "I guess I haven't noticed how much you've changed. And it's true. You have worked hard. You've grown up and you've learned so much. Your dad and I are really proud of you. You deserve something for it. But do you really want to learn more about sheepherding? Maybe it won't be so much fun when we get home."

"Anything I do with Shine would be fun," said Maggie with determination.

"Okay," her mother sighed. "I'll talk to your father. But I'm not promising anything. When we get home, we'll have to have a family meeting to discuss this. We've made some money working up here this summer, and if we come back next year, we'll have to get another pair of dogs. Your father and I thought we wouldn't come back if you didn't like it. But since you do, that changes everything. Next year, you should have a share of the money we make. If you want to spend it then to buy Shine, that's up to you."

A year! Maggie's heart sank right down into her running shoes. So much could happen in a year. A whole year of playing and learning with Shine would be lost. Parents! she thought in frustration. They just never got it no matter how much you tried to tell them.

Chapter Nine

The truck and camper were packed and loaded. "Okay, Maggie," her mother said. "Say goodbye to the mountains. We're on our way to home sweet home."

Reluctantly, Maggie got in the front seat of the truck. Shine jumped in beside her. They drove out of the campsite and started down the long twisting logging road towards the highway far below.

"Goodbye mountains," Maggie thought. "Goodbye, little picas and fat marmots. Goodbye, beautiful lake. Goodbye, cougar and grizzly and elk and deer." She could hardly wait to tell her friends, Ben and Brad, about her summer. What would they think about her almost getting run over by a cougar, about seeing a grizzly, about climbing a mountain peak all by herself? She hadn't told her mother and father about that. It was a memory she wanted to keep to herself. Maybe when she grew up, she could become a famous explorer. She could explore jungles and mountains and far distant oceans. And always at her side would be her faithful dog, Shine. She could just see herself, slipping through the jungle, eyes and ears noticing everything, alert to any danger. Or climbing the highest mountain peaks, fearlessly laughing at difficulties, jumping from rock to rock like a sure-footed mountain goat. And everywhere she went, people would speak of her in hushed tones, "It's Maggie Graham, the great explorer."

It was a long drive home. It was getting dark when the truck finally pulled into their familiar driveway. Maggie jumped out, and ran to give her father, who was waving from the doorway, a big hug.

"C'mon, Shine," she said. "I'll show you my room."

Her room was just as she had left it, the familiar posters on the walls, her desk, her bookcase, her bed. It smelled dusty, but homey too. She flung herself on her bed and patted the covers. Shine jumped up beside her. Maggie thought it would nice to have a nap before supper. But Shine didn't want to relax. She stared at Maggie with her intense brown eyes.

"Shine, just relax," Maggie said, annoyed. "We're home now." But Shine jumped off the bed and began to prowl around the room, sniffing everything. Then she went to the door and whined. Maggie sighed.

"Okay," she said. "We'll go for a walk. But you've got to learn to relax."

They went downstairs and outside. Shine prowled around the yard and then looked at Maggie.

"Okay, okay," she said crossly. She was hungry and tired and she could smell wonderful cooking smells from the kitchen behind her. They went together down the familiar path to the orchard. It was almost dark. Birds were chittering sleepy sounds from the trees. A few crickets were singing in the grass. A warm breeze came and lifted the hair off Maggie's face. The apples on the trees were just starting to get ripe. She found a juicy Gravenstein lying in the grass and bit into it. The tangy juice made her whole body sing. She had forgotten how beautiful her home was, how much she loved the taste of fresh fruit and vegetables from their own garden.

She heard her mom calling from the house.

"Shine," she said, "supper. Let's go eat." Together they ran back to the house, Shine leaping and playing around her in excitement.

There was wonderful food for dinner. Her dad had made the food to celebrate their return. He had roasted a chicken, and made a salad and baked potatoes and even a peach pie for dessert. There were chocolate chip cookies after that.

"Maggie, tomorrow, we have to take Shine back to Bill and Claire's," said her father gently. "Do you want to come along?"

"Yes," said Maggie firmly. "I want to buy Shine."

"Well, Bill has to agree to sell her first," said Len. "She's a valuable dog. We'll see what he says. But don't get your hopes up too high. He might want too much money. He might want to keep her to work on his own farm."

Maggie kept waking up all night to check that Shine was still beside her on the bed. In the morning, she got dressed, had her breakfast, then got in the truck with her father and Shine. Shine followed her everywhere, curled up under her chair while she ate, then jumped in the truck and sat on the seat beside Maggie.

All the way to Bill and Claire's house, Maggie sat folded into a corner of the seat, her arms wrapped around herself, worried about what Bill might say. But Shine sat up on the seat, staring out the window, her eyes eager and intense. When they got to Bill and Claire's, Shine leapt from the truck. She spotted the sheep in the pasture, and immediately went into a crouch, creeping eagerly towards them, body low to the ground, her eyes fixed on the sheep.

"Shine," said Bill, coming out of the house. "That'll do. Come here. Lie down."

Shine did as she was told, but her eyes never left the sheep.

"C'mon in," said Bill. "Coffee's on. Guess there might be some cookies for the little one." Maggie didn't like being called the little one but she trudged behind the two men as they all went in the white farmhouse. Claire was there, setting out cups and a plate of cookies, pouring the coffee and bustling cheerily around the kitchen. The kitchen was full of sunlight, bright yellow curtains on the windows which matched the yellow wallpaper and yellow embroidered tablecloth. There were rows of plants on the windowsills, and a round braided rug on the floor. A wood cookstove in the corner gave out the yeasty smell of baking bread.

"Maggie here has something she wants to talk over with you two," said Len. All the eyes in the room turned to her. For a moment, Maggie was paralysed by fear. Then she realised that Shine was lying on the floor right at her side, and she reached down and patted Shine's warm round head.

"I was wondering..." she said, and hesitated, "well, if you might, that is, if it's okay, I mean, if you want to sell Shine. I know she's valuable and everything and Mom says we don't have much money but she's a really great dog, and well, she's my friend and she saved my life and everything like that." Her last words all came out in a rush.

There was a long silence after she finished. Maggie was afraid to look up. She kept petting Shine. Finally

Bill cleared his throat. "Yep, she's a great little dog, alright," he said. "Hard worker. Smart. Does what she's told. Learns fast." There was another silence.

"Have to think about it," Bill went on after a while. "Might need her this winter. And I was hoping one day to get some puppies from her. Good bloodlines in that dog. Go all the way back to Scotland, they do."

Maggie blinked back tears. It was sounding more and more hopeless.

"Bill," said Claire, firmly. "You stop teasing. You're breaking that girl's heart. Now tell her what you mean and stop stalling."

"Well, I been thinking about all this," said Bill. "I know what it means to want a dog of your own. When I was a kid, I didn't have a dog. I would have done just about anything to get my own dog. Now, I noticed, when I was up there at your camp this summer, that you and this little girl here had formed a special bond. So I kind of wondered what would happen when you folks showed up back here."

Maggie squirmed restlessly on her chair. Bill seemed to take just about forever saying what he meant.

"And then you showed such spunk coming back over the mountains. You were cold and tired but you never complained. You looked out for me and I sure appreciated that. Yep, that made a big impression on me. It sure did."

He paused again. Maggie tried not to squirm.

"But I figured if you were serious about working sheep, you were going to need a little help learning to handle your dog, and of course, she needs to keep working or she'd just plumb curl up and die from boredom. So then I thought about how I could use a little extra help now and again moving sheep around and such. So what say you, young lady, if you come help me work stock on weekends and by next summer, we'll consider this other young lady here your partner?"

Bill sat back on his chair chuckling. Maggie stared. Claire had a big smile on her face. Even her father was grinning.

"You mean..." she gasped.

"Yep," Bill said. "But no fooling around now. When I say work, I mean work. And that means going to the occasional stockdog trial as well. You know what that means, girl?"

"Yes." she said. "Where you and your dog work sheep in a timed contest." She had learned that reading her parent's magazines.

"Hey, you're pretty smart for such a young lady," Bill said. "So now, why don't you take your dog here out for a run and let her get reacquainted with her old home. Rex is down at the barn. Reckon you could go say hello."

"Yes, sir," said Maggie. "And thank you. Thanks so much!"

"Aw, get along now, little lady." said Bill, laughing "but don't forget to take along a cookie or two for

extra supplies. You might get hungry again right smart."

Maggie laughed too, but she grabbed a couple of cookies as she and Shine ran, skipping for joy, out the door.

Chapter Ten

Maggie leapt out of bed. Today was going to be so exciting. She dressed carefully in her best blue jeans and a new purple T-shirt that her mother had bought especially for today. She brushed her hair, her teeth, washed her face, then dashed downstairs to eat breakfast. She was almost too excited to eat. Her mother placed hot cereal, orange juice and toast in front of her. Maggie sighed. She was still homesick for their wonderful lazy breakfasts in the mountains, smoke from the fire slanting up through the trees, the far away sounds of the sheep, and the gentle wind through the cedar trees. She never thought she would miss the place so much, but she did. But being home had its pleasures as well. She loved being back in her own room. She was still glad to be back with her familiar things, her books, her collection of stuffed toys. She was glad to be back at school with her friends. And out by the garage was a brand new shiny-red mountain bike which her dad said she'd earned with all her hard work.

"Are you sure you're ready for today, Maggie?" her mother said. Maggie laughed.

"Sure am," she said. After a summer dealing with bears, cougars, blizzards, lightning and mountain climbing, she thought, making a speech in front a classroom of kids was going to be easy.

After breakfast, she got her books ready, went outside and climbed on her bike. Her friends Ben and

Brad were waiting for her just down the road outside their gate.

"Wow, cool shirt," said Ben. The back of the T-shirt had a picture of an eagle and words that said, "Wild Places, Preserve Them."

They bicycled together through streets of their small town to their school. Brown, gold and red leaves fluttered beside their bikes as they rode. The street was lined with huge trees. The houses were old and comfortable looking. Maggie, Ben and Brad waved to their friends as they rode up to the school. They parked and locked their bikes.

As Maggie went to her classroom and sat down, she was tingling all over, waiting for everyone else to get to their seats and get started. The teacher came in and they waited, as usual, for the announcements to come over the loudspeaker.

Then the teacher said, "Good morning, class. As you know, this morning we are going to be having presentations on the subject of what we did during the summer. This exercise is to practice both writing and speaking. I hope you have all worked hard on your presentations. And now, I would like you to welcome our very first speaker, Maggie Graham."

The class applauded politely. Then they all watched in wonder as Maggie marched to the door of the classroom. "I'll just be a minute," she said politely. "There's someone I need to help me out with my presentation." Then she went into the hall, walked to the front door of the school, and gave a sharp whistle. She came back into the classroom, stood proud and tall at the front of the room.

"Sit, girl," she said, and the black and white collie at her feet sat. Maggie gestured with her hand and Shine lay down. She lay down carefully, for she was still a bit stiff and sore. Shine's bright brown eyes looked steadily at Maggie who took a deep breath and smiled at her dog. Maggie waved her arm and Shine leapt to her feet, injuries forgotten, eyes bright and steady on Maggie's face, ready to go to work.

"My name is Maggie Graham," she said happily, "and this is my border collie, Shine. Well, she's partly mine. And by next summer, she'll be all mine. And we would like to tell you all about the great adventures we had this summer and all the neat things we learned..."

The End

About the Author

LUANNE ARMSTRONG is a BC writer, farmer, and educator. She is presently completing an MFA in Creative Writing at UBC. She writes adult novels, children's books and poetry. Her first two children's books, *Annie*, (Polestar, 1995) and *Arly and Spike*, were Canadian Children's Book Centre selections. Her adult novels include *Bordering* (Gynergy, 1995) and *The Colour of Water* (Caitlin, 1998).

About the Illustrator

DOROTHY WOODEND is an artist, animator, and co-founder of Eponymous Productions and Management Company in Vancouver BC. She has a BA from Simon Fraser University and a BFA from the Emily Carr School of Art and Design. She is a feature writer and illustrator for the Loop Magazine in Vancouver, and teaches children's animation at Arts Umbrella.

If you liked this book...

you might enjoy these other Hodgepog books:

Read them yourself in grades 4-5, or read them to younger kids.

Ben and the Carrot Predicament
by Mar'ce Merrell, illustrated by Barbara Hartmann
ISBN 1-895836-54-9   Price $4.95

Getting Rid of Mr. Ribitus
by Alison Lohans, illustrated by Barbara Hartmann
ISBN 1-895836-53-0   Price $5.95

A Real Farm Girl
by Susan Ioannou, illustrated by James Rozak
ISBN 1-895836-52-2   Price $6.95

A Gift for Johnny Know-It-All
by Mary Woodbury, illustrated by Barbara Hartmann
ISBN 1-895836-27-1   Price $5.95

Mill Creek Kids
by Colleen Heffernan, illustrated by Sonja Zacharias
ISBN 1-895836-40-9   Price $5.95

Arly and Spike
by Luanne Armstrong, illustrated by Chao Yu
ISBN 1-895836-37-9   Price $4.95

A Friend for Mr. Granville
by Gillian Richardson, illustrated by Claudette MacLean
ISBN 1-895836-38-7   Price $5.95

Lost in a Blizzard
by Constance Horne, illustrated by Lori McGregor McCrae
ISBN 1895836-69-7   Price $5.95

Butterfly Gardens
by Judith Benson, Illustrated by Lori McGregor McCrae
ISBN 1-895836-71-9   Price $5.95

and for readers in grades 1-2, or to read to pre-schoolers

Sebastian's Promise
by Gwen Molnar, Illustrated by Kendra McCleskey
ISBN 1-895836-65-4   Price $4.95

Summer With Sebastian
by Gwen Molnar, illustrated by Kendra McCleskey
ISBN 1-895836-39-5   Price $4.95

The Noise in Grandma's Attic
by Judith Benson, illustrated by Shane Hill
ISBN 1-895836-55-7   Price $4.95